The Cityville Times

MORNING EDITION

4th OCTOBER

MORE MONKEY BUSINESS AT CITY ZOO

Middle Park Zoo remains closed today as zookeepers resume efforts to get Beryl, an orangutan, to return the keys to the main gates that she stole two evenings ago.

It has been reported that she distracted her keeper by flinging bananas at him and swiped the keys without him noticing. The theft was only discovered when keepers tried to enter the park yesterday morning, but found themselves locked out.

Since she gained control of the zoo, it has been reported that Beryl has unlocked all the enclosures, gained entry to the food stores, and has got up quite a party atmosphere among her fellow zoo dwellers.

UP! UP! AND AWAY!

A pair of Cityville siblings have flown into the record books after completing a tennis match—in midair!

A pair of Cityville siblings have flown into the record books after completing a tennis match—in midair! Sisters Meredith (57) and Pamela (59) Huffelman from the Upper East Side took to the skies above the city, and completed the full game, set, and match while strapped to the wings of their biplane. Workers in many of the skyscrapers couldn't believe their eyes as the daredevil duo steamed past their windows hitting volley after volley back and forth between them. Their flight lasted approximately 45 minutes with the pair returning to earth in an airfield just outside the city. The sisters have something of a track record for daring stunts—who could forget their tap-dancing routine on a high wire strung between two hot air balloons last year? The sisters are now planning their next exciting challenge. "We're not quite sure what we will do next," said Pamela. "We would like to throw ourselves over a waterfall in a barrel, but we'd need to find our cagoules first."

WOMAN'S GIGANTIC SNEEZE BLOWS HUSBAND'S HAIR OFF

Full story page 4

ESCAPED PRISONERS STILL AT LARGE

Cityville cops are ontinuing to hunt for two risoners who broke free om Cityville County ligh Security Prison two ights ago. Brothers Brian The Brain" and Rory 'Hoolihan, who were oth serving life sentences r their involvement in a ries of very high-profile robberies, are thought to have escaped after tunneling through the wall of their cell using teaspoons, then shimmying down the prison wall using their bedsheets tied together as a rope.

Speaking to our reporter, Police Chief Margie Gunderson believes the brothers are still in the Cityville area. Police ask the public to remain vigilant and if spotted, not to approach the men, but to contact the CPD immediately.

ALEX T. SMITH

Mr. Penguin was a penguin.

If you weren't sure whether he was or not, all you had to do was look at him.

He looked like a penguin.

He was all black and white with a little beak, two flappy flippers—and when he walked, his bottom wiggled about in exactly the sort of way a penguin's bottom should wiggle.

But there was something rather unusual about Mr. Penguin. You see, he wasn't JUST a penguin.

He was an Adventurer!

He had a dashing hat, an enormous magnifying glass, and a battered satchel with a nice packed lunch of fish finger sandwiches inside to prove it.

All he needed now was an adventure to actually go on…

Published by
PEACHTREE PUBLISHERS
1700 Chattahoochee Avenue
Atlanta, Georgia 30318-2112
www.peachtree-online.com

First published in Great Britain in 2017 by Hodder and Stoughton
First United States version published in 2019 by Peachtree Publishers

Artwork created digitally.

Printed in China
10 9 8 7 6 5 4 3 2 1
First Edition
ISBN: 978-1-68263-120-1

Library of Congress Cataloging-in-Publication Data.
Names: Smith, Alex T., author.
Title: Mr. Penguin and the lost treasure / Alex T. Smith.
Description: First edition. | Atlanta : Peachtree Publishers, 2019. | "First published in Great Britain in 2017 by Hodder and Stoughton." | Summary: Aspiring Professional Adventurer Mr. Penguin and his colleague, Colin the spider, try to find a treasure rumored to be buried in The Museum of Extraordinary Objects before bandits do.
Identifiers: LCCN 2018038466 | ISBN 9781682631201
Subjects: | CYAC: Buried treasure—Fiction. | Museums—Fiction. | Robbers and outlaws—Fiction. | Adventure and adventurers—Fiction. | Penguins—Fiction. | Spiders—Fiction. | Mystery and detective stories.
Classification: LCC PZ7.S6422 Mr 2019 | DDC [Fic]—dc23 LC record available at *https://lccn.loc.gov/2018038466*

CONTENTS

1. ALL ADVENTURES CONSIDERED! 9
2. A THOROUGHLY WEDGED BOTTOM 15
3. TO THE MUSEUM! 21
4. CLOSED UNTIL FURTHER NOTICE 27
5. IN A DREADFUL STATE 35
6. WE NEED TO FIND AN X 46
7. THE EARTH MOVES 63
8. A SECRET PASSAGE 69
9. BEWARE THE JUNGLE, DARK AND DEEP 78
10. UNWELCOME GUESTS 89
11. A PECULIAR PROBLEM FOR A PENGUIN 98
12. AN UNEXPECTED ALLIGATOR 107
13. DANGLING ABOVE CERTAIN DEATH 113
14. A SECRET BEHIND THE WATERFALL 120
15. SEVERAL SERIOUS PROBLEMS 131
16. A WRINKLY FACE 139
17. OH BROTHER! 144
18. MR. PENGUIN HAS A PLAN 156
19. HOW NOT TO BE EATEN BY AN ALLIGATOR 162
20. CAUGHT IN THE ACT 169
21. LET'S GET OUTTA HERE! 180
22. A FISH FINGER SANDWICH (AT LAST!) 187
23. HOME 200

CHAPTER ONE

ALL ADVENTURES CONSIDERED!

It was 10:32 AM on a Monday morning, and Mr. Penguin was twirling about slowly on his swizzly office chair and flipping the end of his beak with a crabstick.

He was bored.

OCT
4th

Today was his first day being a Professional Adventurer, but it wasn't quite going to plan. Yesterday, he'd placed an advertisement in the local newspaper, and he'd thought that today his telephone would be ringing its head off from the moment he flipped the CLOSED sign on his office door over to OPEN at 9 AM.

It was supposed to have been nonstop Adventures—people ringing up with mysteries for him to solve, missing diamonds to find, jungles to run through under a shower of poison-tipped darts, and Certain Death to be very much avoided. That sort of thing was always going on in Mr. Penguin's favorite Adventure books, which had given him the idea to be an Adventurer in the first place.

But this hadn't been the case at all.

His telephone had sat tight-lipped and silent. The only noise was the squeak, squeak, squeak of the office chair as Mr. Penguin twirled around, and the low, dreary hum of the fan on the ceiling of Mr. Penguin's igloo.

This really isn't good enough, thought Mr. Penguin, trying not to look at all the unpaid bills pinned to his notice board.

Setting himself up as an Adventurer had been a very expensive business indeed. His special hat with the arrow through it and the selection of rather jazzy bow ties had cost a fortune. And the rent for this igloo was astronomical! All that was left in his piggy bank was a bit of fluff and a paper clip, and the fish finger sandwich in his refrigerator was his very last packed lunch.

If he didn't get an Adventuring job soon, there would be no more fish fingers, no more crabsticks, and a lot more grumbly noises coming from his tummy. It would mean packing up all his belongings into his battered old suitcase and hopping on the first boat back to the Frozen South.

Mr. Penguin shuddered at the memories of stomach-churning waves and icy

winds. "What I need," he said, "is for that phone to ring, and for there to be a jolly exciting Adventure on the other end..."

The words were hardly out of his beak when, would you believe it, the telephone DID ring, and it rang VERY loudly!

CHAPTER TWO

A THOROUGHLY WEDGED BOTTOM

Mr. Penguin was so surprised by the noise that he gasped, tumbled off his chair, and landed in his trash can with a clatter. A few experimental wiggles as he grabbed the telephone receiver told him that his bottom was thoroughly wedged.

"Hello," he said in the most sensible voice he could manage while trying to wrestle his bum out of the can with a flipper. "This is the office of Mr. Penguin, Adventurer *and* Penguin. Mr. Penguin speaking."

"Oh hello, Mr. Penguin!" came a woman's voice from the other end. She sounded rather excited and in a bit of a flap. "Boudicca Bones here," she continued, "owner of the Museum of Extraordinary Objects, and I think you are the person who is going to save me! Mr. Penguin, you are ABSOLUTELY my last hope!"

Mr. Penguin adjusted his bow tie and got ready to listen very carefully—which was rather challenging as he was now spinning around the room, stuck in the paper bin.

"My museum is terribly old and, I'm afraid, it's falling to pieces. Walls are crumbling, doors are falling off their hinges, and yesterday an upstairs toilet dropped through the floor and landed on a very valuable stuffed walrus. The only way we can possibly sort all this out is to find the treasure my great-great-great-grandfather buried somewhere in the museum. My brother and I have looked EVERYWHERE for it. Will you help us? Once the treasure is found, I'll be able to pay you handsomely!"

Mr. Penguin could hardly believe what he was hearing. Falling toilets! Stuffed walruses! Buried treasure! This was it! His first Adventure! AND there was going to be some money for his piggy bank at the end of it too! His flippers were all of a quiver. Of course he wanted to help!

CHAPTER TWO

"I'll be there in a few minutes!" said Mr. Penguin.

"TREMENDOUS!" cried Miss Bones, sounding much happier. "Do please hurry—we simply can't wait!"

CHAPTER THREE

TO THE MUSEUM!

The next five minutes were a blur. Mr. Penguin waddled about as fast as he could, grabbing his hat, his satchel, and his gigantic magnifying glass—all while trying desperately to unwedge his bottom from the waste bin.

Eventually, he grabbed his long-handled shoehorn to crowbar his bottom free. He shot out of the bin like a pinball and went ping-ponging across the room.

Next, he flip-flapped over to the filing cabinet and knocked three times on the third drawer down, which was labeled "COLIN."

No answer.

He tried again, then took matters into his own flippers. He hauled the heavy drawer open, releasing a plume of heavily scented incense smoke into the air. As the smoke cleared, a large spider in a bowler hat became visible, absorbed in a cryptic crossword puzzle.

Mr. Penguin tapped him on the head with his flipper.

"Come on, Colin! We've got—" But that's as far as he got because all of a sudden the spider jerked to attention and grabbed Mr. Penguin's flipper. He hurled him through the air as easily as flipping a pancake, sending Mr. Penguin crashing into the umbrella stand.

"It's ME, Colin!" cried Mr. Penguin, untangling himself from the mess.

Colin blinked a few times and then blushed all the way up to his long, bushy unibrow. He reached under his bowler hat and brought out a notepad and marker pen.

Quickly, he scribbled something on it and showed it to Mr. Penguin.

Then he helped Mr. Penguin up and dusted his knees down for him.

"Don't worry," said Mr. Penguin, slotting his magnifying glass into his satchel and straightening his hat. "But hurry! We are off to the museum for our very first Adventuring job! There's no time to lose!"

And the two friends hurtled out of the room as fast as two stubby, penguin-y legs and eight spindly spider ones could carry them.

A moment later, Mr. Penguin flapped back into his office, dashed to the refrigerator, and grabbed the fish finger sandwich.

CHAPTER THREE

"Almost forgot my packed lunch!" he said, puffing a bit and shoving it into his satchel. "That would NEVER do!"

CHAPTER FOUR

CLOSED UNTIL FURTHER NOTICE

The Museum of Extraordinary Objects was a large, dusty building with lots of tall columns and twirly bits of stonework. It sat on the corner of West 28th Street and Near-the-Park Avenue, and looked, when viewed from one of the surrounding skyscrapers, like a dinosaur.

Mr. Penguin and Colin hoofed it down the road as fast as they could in the rain, weaving in and out of people hopping around puddles being terribly busy and important.

Eventually, Mr. Penguin and Colin rounded a corner and were just making a dash for the gigantic wrought iron museum gates when they crashed smack-bang into an elderly woman buying a newspaper and some birdseed.

"Well, if it isn't Mr. Penguin!" cried the woman. She helped Mr. Penguin up and carefully popped Colin's bowler hat back on his head.

CHAPTER FOUR

It was their good friend Edith Hedge, who lived in the park and fed the birds. Often, Mr. Penguin and Colin would go and share their lunch with her. Edith was, as always, wearing about fifteen different raincoats, one on top of the other, strapped at the waist with a large belt bag. Sitting on top of her head was a pigeon. He was called Gordon.

"And where are my two friends going in such a hurry?" she cried, tossing some bird-seed up to Gordon, who caught it expertly with his beak.

Mr. Penguin puffed out his chest proudly. "We are off to the museum for our first proper Adventuring job. We have to find some buried treasure!"

"Oh dear," said Edith. "I think you might be out of luck—the museum's been closed since yesterday. I've lived in Cityville all my life, and I've never known it to be closed, except on Christmas Day. . .but look! It's shut up tight!" She pointed to the enormous front doors of the museum. A large sign said CLOSED UNTIL FURTHER NOTICE.

"Very strange if you ask me," continued Edith, fussing with her belt bag. "I've known Miss Bones since she was a baby, and she wouldn't close the place unless it was for something *very* serious indeed."

Mr. Penguin was a bit confused. He looked down at Colin, who shrugged as many of his shoulders as he could manage without falling over. This was most odd. Why would Miss Bones call him to the museum if it was closed?

"Oh, I know what must be going on!" he cried with a flash of inspiration. "I bet Miss Bones and her brother closed the museum to look for the treasure without lots of people getting in the way. That has got to be it!"

Edith's face creased up into a smile. It was like looking at a very friendly, crinkled paper bag. "Well, there we are!" she said. "That must be what's happening. You ARE clever, Mr. Penguin. Now, promise you'll come and find me as soon as you can to tell me about this treasure."

"Of course!" said Mr. Penguin. "But now we must go—we're running a bit late." He straightened his hat, tweaked his bow tie, and started off toward the front doors of the museum with Colin scampering madly behind him.

CHAPTER FOUR

"Good luck!" cried Edith, waving her newspaper at them. Gordon ruffled his feathers encouragingly. The two of them headed back into the park as Mr. Penguin and Colin clambered up the steps of the museum.

CHAPTER FIVE

IN A DREADFUL STATE

The gigantic doors of the museum were flung open before Mr. Penguin could even knock the knocker or ring the bell. He and Colin were ushered into the entrance hall by a terribly efficient woman who shut the doors tight again, locked them, and flung the large iron key into her handbag with a nervous, wobbly hand.

Only then did she turn around and Mr. Penguin and Colin got their first look at Miss Boudicca Bones. She was a Woman of a Certain Age and was nearly as wide as she was tall. In fact, she was much like a beach ball on legs—a beach ball wearing a neat little pair of pumps and a pussy bow blouse in powdered shrimp.

She was obviously in a terrible flap, but her big red lips broke into a wide, relieved smile when she'd finished fiddling with the clasp on her handbag.

"Mr. Penguin! My knight in shining armor!" she cried, as she led them out of the shadows and into the atrium with its

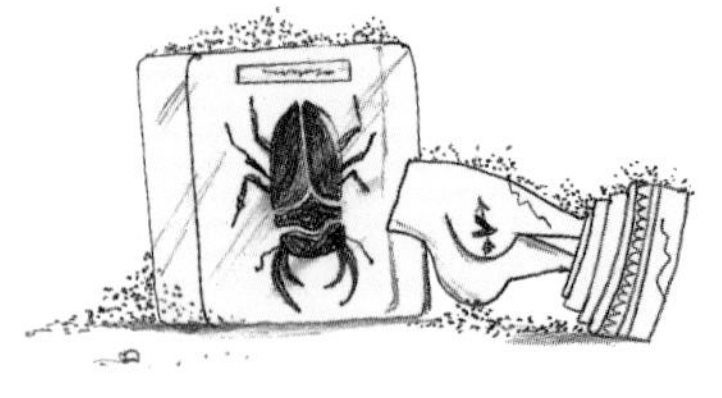

domed glass ceiling. "Thank GOODNESS you're here! Just look at the state of the place. I mean, just LOOK! It's falling apart at the seams!"

Mr. Penguin and Colin stopped and looked around them. Miss Bones was right! The museum was in a dreadful state. Great chunks of plaster had crumbled off the walls, framed pictures and notices had fallen off their hooks, and everything—including the gigantic dinosaur skeleton in the center of the room—was covered in a layer of dust so thick it looked like it had been snowing indoors.

It had been years since Mr. Penguin

had last visited the museum, and he remembered it as warm and sunny and full of people. But now, without any visitors and with a mess everywhere, it was silent and shadowy and ever so slightly spooky.

"What on earth happened?" gasped Mr. Penguin.

"Age, I'm afraid," said Miss Bones sadly. "The museum is well over two hundred years old, you see, and when one thing goes, everything else simply follows. It started with some tiles slipping off the roof, and now…all this."

Great big tears bubbled up behind her spectacles, and she fished down the front

of her blouse for a lace-edged hanky. She dabbed at her eyes before blowing her nose loudly in it. It sounded like a foghorn.

"What my dear relatives would say if they could see it like this, I don't know… They'd be so disappointed in me…," she sighed.

Just then, the biggest man Mr. Penguin and Colin had ever seen came out of an upstairs room. He made his way down the staircase that wound around the atrium like a snail's shell. He must have been at least seven feet tall and was squeezed into pinstripe slacks and a tie that looked like it was attempting to strangle him. He placed

a hand the size of a frying pan on Miss Bones's shoulder and patted it gently.

"This is my brother, Montague," croaked Miss Bones in her husky voice. "We're both so glad you came to help us. Finding the lost treasure my great-great-great-grandpapa buried really is our last hope of fixing all this damage to the museum and bringing it back to its former glory. Without it, I'm afraid we'll be finished."

You're not the only ones, thought Mr. Penguin grimly. His mind wandered to the bills piling up at his igloo, and the damp, drafty boat he'd be stuck on for weeks on the long journey back to the Frozen South.

He shook the thoughts from his head and stuck out his chest again. "Don't you worry," he said, "we'll sort all this out. We'll find the treasure for you!" He flashed his best smile.

Colin wasn't quite so confident, but he smiled anyway.

"I certainly hope so!" said Miss Bones, stashing away her hanky. "Now let me show you the clues we've found already." She led them all upstairs.

Mr. Penguin waddled alongside her, bursting with excitement. A real treasure hunt! With clues! This was BRILLIANT!

Colin followed behind, frowning to himself. Something about this empty museum was making him feel a bit goose-bumpy. It was as if they were being watched…

CHAPTER SIX

WE NEED TO FIND AN X

"Well, here we are!" said Miss Bones, gesturing to a table full of objects in her office.

It had obviously been a very nice room once—quite a fancy affair with neat bookshelves and little lace doilies on all the side tables. Now, like the rest of the museum, it was falling apart. Books were stacked up in huge piles, most of the shelves were hanging off the walls, and the lace doilies looked like they had been rummaged through at a particularly energetic yard sale.

Mr. Penguin clambered up a handy pile of books so he could get a proper look at everything on the table. Colin threw out a length of cobweb, twirled it above his head like a lasso, and used it to climb up beside his friend.

“These,” continued Miss Bones, “are the clues we’ve found already. Montague and I have spent the last day or so hunting by ourselves, haven’t we, Monty?”

Monty grunted and nodded his head. Obviously the strong, silent type—a bit like Colin, thought Mr. Penguin.

"We started here!" said Miss Bones, pointing to a book called *A History of the Museum of Extraordinary Objects.* "It was written ages ago by some relative of mine, and it mentions the buried treasure. Most people, including myself, thought it was all just a story, but I did a bit more research and discovered that there could be something to it. A scroll tucked away in a hidden drawer on my desk here led us to a carved saber-toothed ostrich tusk in one of the second-floor galleries, which in turn sent

us to look at that stuffed walrus I mentioned earlier on the phone. We found a little word search puzzle tucked away in his armpit just before the toilet fell through the roof. Rather lucky really..."

As she talked, Mr. Penguin listened carefully and stroked his beak with a flipper in what he hoped looked like a clever and very thoughtful gesture.

"Montague was no help at all with the word search puzzle, but I did it quite quickly. It gave us the clue 'X MARKS THE SPOT' but, to tell you the truth, we are now stumped! We've looked for crosses here, there, and everywhere—even behind the family portraits and under the trees in the courtyard..."

Mr. Penguin cast an eye out of a nearby window and gasped.

"Awful as it was," said Miss Bones, fussing with her blouse, "the storm last week that ripped them all out of the ground did us a favor. It meant Monty could look for clues

all around them—roots and all. He's going to plant them all back this weekend, aren't you, dear?"

Monty hadn't really been listening, he'd been picking at a fingernail, but hearing his name made him jump and nod his head vigorously.

Miss Bones beamed at Mr. Penguin and blinked expectantly behind her spectacles.

"You'll be able to find the X, won't you?" she asked.

But Mr. Penguin didn't have a clue. He flipped through *A History of the Museum of Extraordinary Objects* and found an illustrated map at the back.

NEAR-THE-PARK AVE
The Museum of Extraordinary Objects
Nr-the-Park Ave Cityville 080427
Floor Plan: Ground Floor
PERIMETER WALL
SIDE GATE (LOCKED)
SIR RANDOLPH BONES'S INSECT RESEARCH LAB - (AND CAFE) -
SIR ANGUS HOLLICK'S AMAZING ARBORETUM
STAIRCASE TO UPPER FLOORS AND OFFICES
THE MUSEUM OF EXTRAORDINARY OBJECTS
GLASS-DOMED ENTRANCE HALL
TICKET HALL
MAIN GATE
TOILET
TOILET
JANITOR'S CUPBOARD
DUCK POND
THE S.R. THOMAS LIBRARY OF UNWRITTEN BOOKS
BARONESS VON CLONKER'S HALL OF WIGS
LADY PERDU'S MYSTERY MAZE
OLD WELL
CAFE
NOT SO HELPFUL POINT
HELP POINT
GIFT SHOP
COLLECTION OF STATUES MISSING NOSES
NOSES FALLEN FROM STATUES
COLLECTION OF ODD SMELLS
MAIN HALLWAY
- HOME OF SIR EDWARD FARQUARHARSON'S MECHANICAL MARVELS -
COLLECTION OF DOORS THAT LEAD NOWHERE
INTERESTING AND UNUSUAL TEA AND COFFEEPOTS
The Museum of
- Extraordinary Objects -
Over 750,000 EXTRAORDINARY objects displayed on seven floors!
Cityville's Oldest Museum!
AERIAL VIEW OF THE MUSEUM
- THE GRAND ATRIUM -
ANCIENT MASKS THAT MAY OR MAY NOT BE HAUNTED
HALL OF UNRELIABLE TRAPDOORS
MADAME AGNES ENNUI MEMORIAL - LECTURE - THEATRE
LOST PROPERTY COLLECTION

"I suggest," he said, playing for time, "that we start our hunt at the very top of the museum and don't stop until we've found it. We could split up into two groups to be quicker." Mr. Penguin was hoping he might be able to slip off somewhere to have a sneaky bite of his fish finger sandwich. It was past lunchtime now, and his stomach was telling him so rather loudly.

"Excellent," Miss Bones said, "but I'd rather we all stick together."

Mr. Penguin's stomach groaned, but he disguised the sound by whooping loudly and enthusiastically, and they all set off.

Colin leapt expertly from Mr. Penguin's shoulder and did a survival roll across the floor tiles. Just as he was about to follow everyone down the corridor, he stopped. He'd heard something. What was it?

It sounded like hammering or a distant thumping somewhere—as if someone was outside and knocking at a heavy door to come in.

Colin cocked his head to listen more carefully, but, as he did, the knocking noise stopped.

He reached under his bowler hat, pulled out his pad and pen, and wrote HMMM. And he underlined it VERY importantly.

For the next twenty minutes they hunted high and low. They looked down all the chimneys and in all the air vents.

PSST

They searched around stone statues and inspected tribal masks. They looked inside huge painted vases and behind boxes of souvenir postcards in the store cupboard.

On the ground floor, in a room devoted to Interesting and Unusual Tea and Coffeepots, Colin heard that strange clonking noise again. He tapped Mr. Penguin on the kneecap and held up his little notebook.

PSST, it said.

Mr. Penguin looked around. Miss Bones and Montague were removing a large teapot from the wall and were quite distracted.

"Yes?" he hissed.

CHAPTER SIX

Colin flipped over the page on his notebook.

CAN YOU HEAR THAT BANGING NOISE?

Mr. Penguin cocked his head and listened. There was indeed an odd banging sort of noise coming from somewhere.

I DON'T LIKE IT, said Colin's pad. I THINK SOMEONE IS TRYING TO BREAK IN.

Mr. Penguin listened again. The banging stopped.

"Don't be silly!" he said. "Who would want to break in? The front door has that big CLOSED sign on it, so everyone knows the museum isn't open. It's probably the pipes. Old buildings like this always have noisy, clonky pipes!"

Colin wasn't convinced, but before he could scribble anything else, Miss Bones sighed loudly and said, "Nothing in here. Let's carry on, although we do seem to be running out of places."

Colin popped his pad away, and the four treasure hunters continued their search.

Fifteen minutes later they were back in the entrance hall, and everyone sagged and looked depressed.

"No X anywhere!" huffed Miss Bones, pursing her lips.

Mr. Penguin scratched his head. "If we were on a desert island looking for PIRATE treasure," he said half to himself, "there would be a great big X on the floor for us to find. But there isn't one here at—" He stopped. Just a minute, he thought. What if there WAS an X on the floor of the museum and it had been there all along and none of them had noticed it?

He opened the book and scoured the map again before tapping it joyfully with a flipper.

"There IS an X!" he cried. "Look!"

He pointed to the part of the map showing the circular entrance hall. There was the dinosaur skeleton in the middle, and all the way around the edge of the room the words "THE MUSEUM OF EXTRAORDINARY OBJECTS" had been carved into the floor.

"AND," cried Mr. Penguin, "the word 'EXTRAORDINARY' has an X in it!"

Everyone gasped.

"What if..." continued Mr. Penguin, "... that X is where the treasure is hidden? Let's go and have a look!"

But the four treasure hunters didn't

have far to go at all. As luck would have it, Mr. Penguin was, right at that very moment, standing directly on top of the enormous X. The X that possibly marked the spot.

CHAPTER SEVEN

THE EARTH MOVES

Before you could say "Crabsticks!" Mr. Penguin had whipped out his gigantic magnifying glass and was scouring every last inch of the large carved letter. When he got to the exact center, where the two lines crossed, he gently ran his flipper over the surface.

"THERE!" he cried, huffing away a thick layer of dust. "Look! There's a little button!"

Everyone bustled around to take a look. Indeed, there was a small button set into the stonework.

Mr. Penguin held his breath and pressed the button.

Nothing happened.

He tried it again, this time pressing harder, and when it didn't do anything, he slapped it with his flipper.

Nothing happened.

Miss Bones had a go, prodding it with one of her fat, little sausage fingers. That didn't work either.

"Monty, darling," she said, cleaning her specs on her blouse, "could you try? There's a lamb..."

Monty cracked his knuckles (which sounded like a wooden fence breaking in a tornado) and knelt down next to the X. He pressed the button. Then he pressed it again.

Nothing.

He smacked it with his fist, stamped on it with his shoe, grunted, and hurried off to the nearby janitor's cupboard to grab a sledgehammer.

He was just raising the hammer above his head when Colin tapped him politely on the ankle and held up his notepad.

It said ALLOW ME.

Everyone stepped back and watched as Colin took the floor. He scuttled over to the button and carefully observed it for a few seconds. Then he pressed four of his feet together and bowed respectfully. He took a deep breath, narrowed his eyes, and…

He kicked the button with a ferocious kung fu kick!

"Well, I can't see that doing any good!" sniffed Miss Bones, but the floor beneath her feet began to tremble. Soon, everything was wobbling about like a plate full of jelly. The dinosaur skeleton rattled, and all the glass in the domed ceiling began to jangle.

"WHAT'S HAPPENING?!" cried Miss Bones, clasping her cardigan about her chest.

Mr. Penguin was just about to yell that he wasn't actually sure, when the X on the ground started to sink, and, as it did, the entire floor of the entrance hall rotated. This was accompanied by the most almighty grumbling sound of stone grinding against stone.

CHAPTER SEVEN

A gust of hot, stale air gushed out of the hole in the floor, and the first few narrow steps of a stone staircase came into view.

CHAPTER EIGHT

A SECRET PASSAGE

A few moments later, the rotating stopped, and the sound of enormous metal bolts sliding into place ricocheted around the room.

Then there was silence.

Miss Bones, Monty, Mr. Penguin, and Colin all stood looking at the black void into which the staircase disappeared.

"What do we do now?" whispered Miss Bones, quivering.

Mr. Penguin swallowed and adjusted his bow tie. He didn't really know. The hero in his favorite Adventure books would have leapt eagerly (and often head first) into the darkness without a second thought.

Mr. Penguin was having second thoughts, though. And third ones. But you're an Adventurer, Mr. Penguin, he said to himself. Be BRAVE!

"I suppose we go down there," he said aloud (and only slightly nervously).

"Fabulous!" said Miss Bones. "Off you go then. We'll wait here for you."

Mr. Penguin paused with one leg in the air. "Aren't you coming with us?"

Miss Bones stared at him, horrified. "Me?!" she gasped. "Go down THERE? But there could be all manner of who-knows-what waiting to pounce. I…er… should um…stay up here and look after the museum…"

"No one's going to come to the Museum—it's closed, remember?" said Mr. Penguin. "Anyway, we need you to come with us to help find the treasure. Four brains are better than two!"

Miss Bones chewed her lip. She glanced up at her giant brother who was looking a bit pale and green around the edges. Then she sighed. "Very well," she huffed. "But you'll have to help me down those steps in this pencil skirt. . ."

And so all four of them set off.

After the first few steps they were plunged into complete and utter darkness. Great curtains of ancient cobwebs wafted into their faces, and the walls seemed to hiss and jiggle in the blackness.

There was some brief rustling as Montague patted himself down to find his box of matches. He scraped one against his stubbly chin, and a tiny orange flame flared. The Adventurers recoiled in horror—the walls and floor were all teeming with strange bugs and creepy-crawlies that jumped from their hiding places and onto the gang. Montague squealed, and the match blew out with a puff.

FANCY LIVING DOWN HERE IN THIS MOLDY OLD TUNNEL, thought Colin, WHEN THEY COULD BE LIVING JUST A FEW BLOCKS AWAY

CHAPTER EIGHT

IN A NICE, QUIET FILING CABINET LIKE I DO…

They hurried on as quickly as they could, each step taking them deeper and deeper under the museum. Every few moments

Miss Bones screamed when she felt something wiggle up her stockings.

The tunnel started to become warmer and the walls slimy and slippery. Some of the steps were now quite uneven, and it was difficult to keep walking without falling over—especially if you were trying to negotiate them on two stubby, penguin-y legs…

All this, together with Miss Bones's yelps and screams, had Mr. Penguin's heart banging in his chest—as loudly as the marching band's drums in Cityville's annual Christmas Parade. Mr. Penguin had thought they would have found the treasure by now and that he would be sitting in the park with Colin, telling Edith Hedge all about it. Adventuring was a lot more dangerous than he'd imagined.

If only, he thought, I could stop and have a bite of my nice sandwich. That really would make me feel much, much braver.

Just as he imagined licking his beak happily, behind him, Miss Bones' feet went out from under her, and she thumped down several steps. She grabbed wildly to steady herself, and her handbag accidentally whacked against the wall. It must have hit a hidden lever because, with a heavy clonk, the steps underneath them merged together to create a slime-covered chute.

They all crashed into each other like pins in a bowling alley and shot down the slide at breakneck speed.

"AAAAARRRRRGH!" they all yelled, terrified.

Then they turned a corner sharply and were hurled like cannonballs out into the air...

BUMP! CRASH! WALLOP!

They hit the ground and skidded along on their bottoms over roasting hot, sandy earth.

CHAPTER NINE

BEWARE THE JUNGLE, DARK AND DEEP

Mr. Penguin was the first on his feet. He dusted himself off, plonked his hat back on his head, and looked around, blinking. He couldn't believe his eyes.

They were now in a vast open space as high as a cathedral and as hot as a pizza oven. All around them great, green trees grew from the ferny undergrowth. It was a thick, jungly rainforest, hung all about with ropes of tangled vines. Jewel-colored butterflies and fireflies with glowing bottoms fluttered and buzzed around their heads.

Miss Bones scrabbled to her feet, followed by Montague and Colin. Everyone was covered from head to toe in a mixture of slimy mud, dusty cobwebs, and sand.

"Where…where are we?" gasped Miss Bones, her eyes as big as dinner plates.

Mr. Penguin hadn't a clue, so he consulted the book again. "According to the

map," he said, "we should be in the museum basement. But this doesn't look like the basement to me!"

"And the treasure is hidden down here?" asked Miss Bones eagerly.

"I suppose it must be!" said Mr. Penguin, rubbing his beak thoughtfully. "But where?"

The answer came from Colin. He tapped Mr. Penguin on the knee and pointed at a nearby tree. Carved into the trunk, slightly mossy with age, was an arrow. It pointed downward.

The treasure hunters gingerly made their way through the foliage toward it. When they reached the tree they looked down. There was nothing to see other than sandy soil.

Mr. Penguin took out his magnifying glass and spotted the corner of something wooden slightly sticking out of the earth.

"What's this?" he cried. He started to dig with his flippers, and with the help of Montague's enormous hands, they soon uncovered a wooden box.

Mr. Penguin tried to open the lid, but it was stuck fast. He nodded at Colin, who grinned, and with another kung fu KA-POW! the lid went flying. Inside was a hand-drawn map and a very old-looking envelope sealed with red wax and stamped with two crossed bones.

"The family crest," whispered Miss Bones.

Mr. Penguin opened the envelope and read the message inside.

BEWARE THE JUNGLE,
DARK AND DEEP.
FOR IN THE SHADOWS
CREATURES CREEP
WITH JAWS THAT GNASH
AND TEETH THAT BITE.
OH YES, MY CHUMS,
THEY'RE QUITE A SIGHT!

SO FOLLOW THIS MAP,
IT LEADS TO RICHES.
BUT UNWISE IS HE
WHO FROM THE PATH SWITCHES.

Sir Randolph Bones

FOUNDER OF THE MUSEUM
AND PROFESSIONAL TREASURE HUNTER

Mr. Penguin opened the map up carefully, and everyone gathered around to look. A red dotted line wove its way across the page, twisting and turning around trees and boulders. It went over what looked like several rope bridges hanging above deep valleys and a river with a waterfall. It ended at another X.

"All this was hiding under the museum all along?" asked Mr. Penguin. "And you didn't know anything about it?"

"Nothing at all!" said Miss Bones, and from the look on her face, Mr. Penguin could tell she was as bamboozled as the rest of them.

Mr. Penguin straightened his hat and took a step forward. The quicker they found this treasure, the quicker he would be able to eat his fish finger sandwich.

He followed the red line on the map, which led to an overgrown path between two enormous palm trees. Everyone fell in behind him, and the troupe of treasure hunters began making their way, at last, to the treasure.

It was a difficult trek. There was a lot of clambering over fallen tree trunks and fighting through tangled foliage that slapped against their faces. Mr. Penguin found it quite tricky to remain the right way up and not trip over the many sudden bumps and lumps underfoot. Soon, Colin took the lead, on account of his kung fu kicking legs being rather handy at breaking through branches.

They were just stopping for a breather in a small clearing when Colin suddenly stopped.

LISTEN! he wrote on his pad. Then on the next page:

LISTEN TO THAT!

Everyone stopped and strained their ears. The strange noise from earlier had returned, but this time there was no doubt whatsoever about what it was: FOOTSTEPS. And they weren't terribly far away.

CHAPTER NINE

"Sounds like someone is following us!" whispered Mr. Penguin, fussing nervously with his bow tie.

Miss Bones gasped and clasped a hand to her bosom. Her eyes darted toward Montague, and they both went pale.

"I think I know who it is!" she hissed, grasping on to her brother with her plump, trembling hands. "Jewel thieves!"

CHAPTER TEN

UNWELCOME GUESTS

Miss Bones, Mr. Penguin, Monty, and Colin began hotfooting it through the jungle as best they could while listening to Miss Bones's story.

"You see," she said, hitching her skirt up above her knees to maneuver over a large, mossy rock, "I fear we might not be the only ones after the treasure. That's why we called you in so urgently—it's vital that we find the treasure today so it doesn't fall into their hands."

The rope bridge below them started to buckle and creak ominously as Montague Bones hefted his gigantic feet over it. Mr. Penguin peeked over the edge and immediately wished he hadn't. It was an awfully long way to fall if he slipped.

"I don't know whether you've been following the story in the newspaper over the last few days," Miss Bones continued as they all stumbled along the next bit of fern-covered pathway, "but two crooks have escaped from the local prison. Brian and Rory O'Hoolihan—brothers and notorious jewel thieves!"

Mr. Penguin and Colin both nodded grimly. They'd read the news articles and had decided they sounded like a thoroughly dreadful pair.

"Well, I believe," said Miss Bones, "that they have escaped for one reason and one reason only: to steal the museum's treasure!"

Before Mr. Penguin could reply, he tripped over and fell face first into a small hole in the ground. Miss Bones and

Montague heaved him out of it, while Colin circled them with four of his legs up, ready to leap into kung fu action if they were pounced upon by a wild creature or a jewel thief or two.

"Why didn't you tell us?" said Mr. Penguin, when he'd blown his beak into his hanky to get rid of all the soil he'd inhaled. If he'd known at the start about the possibility of two hulking great jewel thieves—real, DANGEROUS CRIMINALS— following them, he would have phoned the police.

Miss Bones looked down at her feet and twizzled her handbag straps nervously between her fingers.

"Well, to be perfectly honest with you, Mr. Penguin," she said, blushing, "I didn't tell you because I'm so embarrassed about it all. I was worried you'd think I'd encouraged them..."

As the gang of treasure hunters began moving again, Miss Bones explained.

"Brian O'Hoolihan has been writing to me from prison for some time, usually asking questions about objects in the museum. He was doing some sort of history course to better himself, and I was keen to help," puffed Miss Bones as they continued through the jungle. "He must have read about the legend of the treasure in a copy of *A History of the Museum of Extraordinary Objects* from the prison library, and he started asking me about it. That made me concerned, and I stopped writing back. Then I read in the newspaper that they had escaped from prison, and I was certain they'd come for the treasure! That's when I asked Monty to come and

stay with me—partly for protection, but mainly to help me find the treasure and get it somewhere safe. When we couldn't find it, we called you in. But now it seems they've been spying on us and are following us to it. It's all my fault! If I hadn't replied to Brian in the first place, we wouldn't be in this mess. We have to find that treasure first!"

They came to a teetering halt at the bank of an underground river, which was flowing really quite fast.

CHAPTER TEN

Mr. Penguin was looking frantically at the treasure map. Something wasn't right. "We've come the wrong way!" he hollered, his flippers all of a fluster. "We shouldn't be by the river! We'll have to turn back!"

As they turned to do so, a piercing squawk went up, and a flock of startled birds took to the air. They flew as fast as they could into the dark, vaulted heights above.

"The O'Hoolihan brothers!" gasped Miss Bones. "They can't be too far away! We'll have to go over the river!"

Mr. Penguin, with his heart pounding in his head and his bow tie all askew, looked at the map again. There wasn't a bridge nearby.

He looked at the fast-flowing waters and glanced at Colin. Colin nodded. There was only one thing to do—if they couldn't go over the river, they'd have to go through it!

Mr. Penguin gulped. There was only one problem with that. He didn't really know how to swim…

CHAPTER ELEVEN

A PECULIAR PROBLEM FOR A PENGUIN

"But you're a penguin!" cried Miss Bones when he told her. "How can you not know how to swim?"

"Well, I can sort of paddle about a bit," said Mr. Penguin, his shoulders sagging, "but I wouldn't be very good in all this water here…"

Again, a vision of being stuck on a rickety old boat on the way back to the Frozen South bobbed into Mr. Penguin's mind. Freezing seawater everywhere. Awful!

Miss Bones pursed her lips for a moment. "Monty, you'll have to carry them," she said to her brother who was still staring eagerly at Mr. Penguin. "What about the spider? Can he swim?"

"Oh, wonderfully so!" beamed Mr. Penguin. "He's like a goldfish! Even without his swimming cap—he's left that at home…"

Colin flashed a cheerful grin.

That was settled then. Colin flexed his legs to get ready to battle the river's current, and Miss Bones gathered herself ready for a dip in the rushing river.

They were just about to clamber down the bank to the water when Mr. Penguin spotted something…

"Look! A log!"

And indeed it was! A large log—more like a big, knobbly tree trunk—was floating toward them. It slowed down to a stop right by their feet.

"Perfect!" Mr. Penguin cried. "We can

sit on this and paddle across the river to the other side. The map says we aren't really that far from the treasure. This will be a shortcut!"

AND WE WON'T GET OUR FEET WET, added Colin helpfully.

They all tiptoed onto the log and sat down gingerly. The knobblyness made it a bit uncomfortable, especially as it rocked and wobbled in the water.

Monty pushed off from the bank, and they went splashing into the river. The current pushed them sideways, but Monty used his enormous hands to paddle, and they slowly started to make their way across to the opposite bank. It was actually rather easy—almost like the log was swimming through the water itself.

Miss Bones concentrated on not losing her balance and sitting as ladylike as possible without toppling over into the river and flashing her knickers.

Colin skittered to the front to keep lookout, and Mr. Penguin buried his beak in the treasure map, looking at where they should be going.

"Yes!" he shouted over the noise of the water. "We're really close to the treasure now. I wonder why this map was telling us to go the long way around instead of just crossing the river?"

Colin tapped him on the knee.

"Hang on, Colin!" said Mr. Penguin, not looking up from the map. "I'm busy investigating. Once we get to the other

side, we'll practically be on top of the treasure. Colin, I said, HANG ON!"

Colin had tapped him on the knee again.

"Any second now," continued Mr. Penguin, "we'll be able to hop off this log and cut through those plants on the other side, clamber up to this cave, and find the treas—WHAT IS IT, COLIN? WHY DO YOU KEEP TAPPING ME?"

Mr. Penguin finally looked up and glared at his friend.

Colin had his pad out. It said I DON'T THINK THIS IS A LOG.

"Don't be silly, Colin," chuckled Mr. Penguin. "Of course it's a log! What else could it be?"

Colin scribbled on his pad.

I THINK IT MIGHT BE AN ALLIGATOR.

He flipped it over to a fresh sheet.

A REALLY BIG ALLIGATOR.

Mr. Penguin laughed. "Oh, Colin! You really are a silly sausage sometimes!" And he turned to Miss Bones, and they both started to giggle. However, a second later they stopped abruptly at the sight in front of them.

CHAPTER ELEVEN

An enormous alligator's head had emerged from the water. It looked over its shoulder and grinned a gigantic, toothy, terrifying grin.

CHAPTER TWELVE

AN UNEXPECTED ALLIGATOR

There was absolutely no doubt about it—they were DEFINITELY sitting on the knobbly back of an enormous alligator who appeared to be VERY hungry indeed!

For a few moments no one did anything, then everyone did everything very quickly.

The alligator began thrashing about wildly in the water.

Montague leapt into the river with a strangled yelp and tried to swim away.

Miss Bones screamed and tried to stand up on the alligator's back to run, but she slipped, scrambled about in midair for a few seconds, then splashed into the water.

Mr. Penguin shoved the map into his satchel and joined her.

Colin calmly popped his pad back under his bowler hat and narrowed his eyes. Judging the moment just right, he ran down the alligator's snout and biffed it right on the nose.

The alligator snapped its jaws and roared, but Colin was too quick. He leapt over the beast's mouth, giving it another good bop on the snout mid-jump. Then he splashed into the water and swam as quickly as he could toward Mr. Penguin.

He wasn't a moment too soon!

Poor Mr. Penguin was desperately trying to keep his satchel with the map and his sandwich in it above the water. Colin reached him and held on to one of Mr. Penguin's flippers, which gave Mr. Penguin the confidence to start treading water with his feet.

"I KNEW THAT I SHOULD HAVE PACKED MY FLOATIES!" he cried over the roaring sounds of the river and the chomp, chomp, chomp of the alligator's jaws as it gnashed toward them.

"What do we do now?" called Miss Bones, clambering up onto her brother's enormous shoulders.

Mr. Penguin tried to think—which was very hard when faced with an extremely hungry alligator. But the alligator had stopped gnashing its jaws and was glaring over the Adventurers' shoulders at something behind them. It yelped, twisted around, and swam madly against the flow of the river.

"What is it doing now?" cried Mr. Penguin. With Colin's help he splashed around and saw what had frightened the beast. They were all rapidly heading toward a—

"WATERFALL!!!" shouted Mr. Penguin. "WE'RE HEADING TOWARD A WATER-FALL!!"

Everyone turned to look in horror at the river falling away into nothingness. Before he could do anything, Mr. Penguin was thrown over its watery edge.

CHAPTER THIRTEEN

DANGLING ABOVE CERTAIN DEATH

Mr. Penguin felt his tummy lurch with the topsy-turvy, wobbly-jelly feeling of flying through the air as he hurtled toward the sharp rocks in the lagoon below.

Then, suddenly, it all stopped.

Instead of falling, Mr. Penguin now found himself…dangling?

He looked up. By some wonderful stroke of luck, the strap of his satchel had tangled around a branch that jutted out through the waterfall. As Mr. Penguin gripped his satchel with his flippers, he saw Colin come tumbling toward him.

"QUICK, COLIN!" shouted Mr. Penguin over the noise of the rushing water. "GRAB ON TO ME!"

Colin didn't need to hear that twice. He fired out a rope of webbing and lassoed Mr. Penguin's belly. Then he swung toward

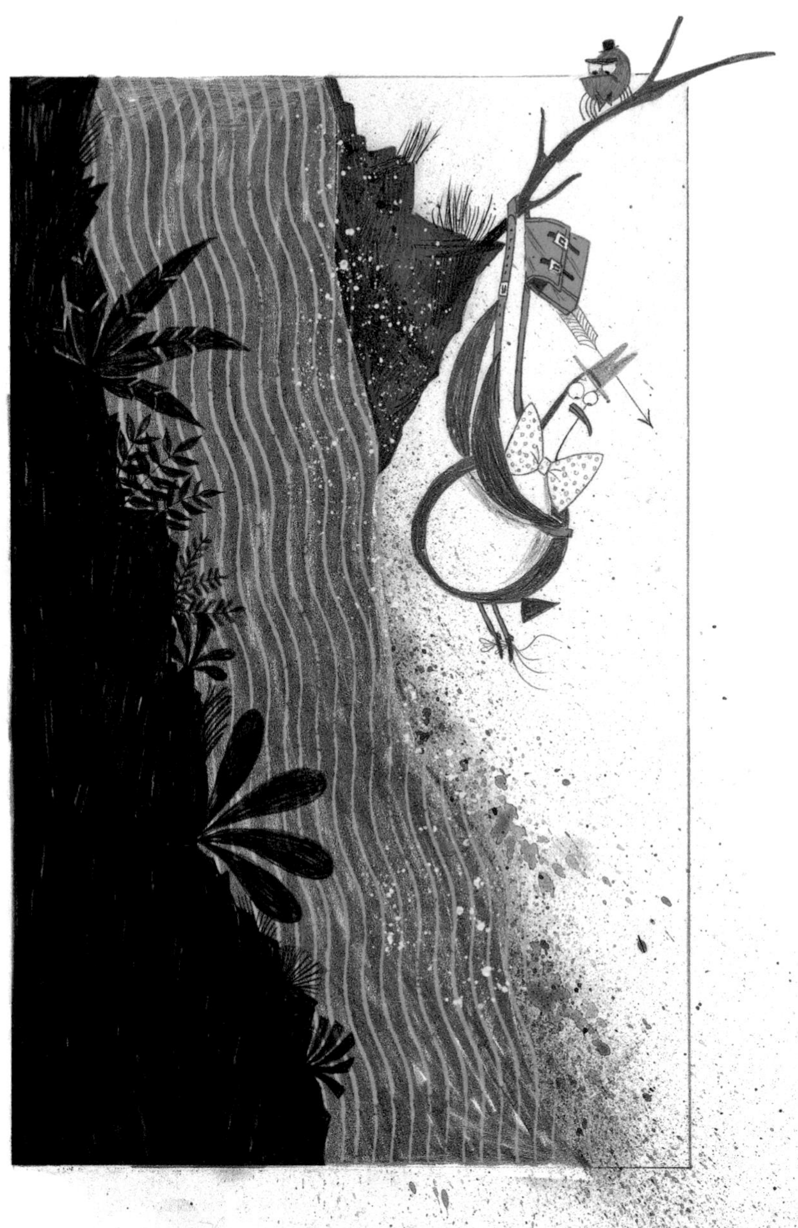

his friend and clambered up and over his beak, onto the satchel and onto the branch. He was safe.

Miss Bones came flying past next, throwing her arms out and catching Mr. Penguin's feet. She dangled, huffing and puffing and holding on with all her might.

Montague quickly followed—at first gripping on to his sister's ample waist before slipping down to her ankles. Above their heads, the strap of Mr. Penguin's satchel groaned.

Finally, the alligator flew over their heads and splashed into the churning waters below. Everyone looked down and gasped. The beast disappeared for a moment before its head burst through the water. It blinked for a few seconds before gnashing its jaws again. Mr. Penguin gulped. From the shadowy depths, more alligators appeared, circling around and grinding their teeth.

Mr. Penguin looked up at the satchel and the branch. What was he going to do? Miss Bones and her brother were REALLY heavy, and he wouldn't be able to hold on much longer. The seams of his satchel were slowly pinging apart, and he could feel the ancient branch above starting to move.

"HURRY AND DO SOMETHING, MR. PENGUIN!" squealed Miss Bones from somewhere around his ankles.

"WE'RE GOING TO BE EATEN BY THOSE MONSTERS!"

Mr. Penguin gritted his beak and tried to twist his flippers around his satchel strap to haul himself upward. But it was useless. The branch above him began to creak and groan.

On the branch, Colin whipped out his notepad and wrote GASP!

Mr. Penguin squeezed his eyes shut and prepared to be gobbled up by the creatures below.

CHAPTER FOURTEEN

A SECRET BEHIND THE WATERFALL

A full minute passed and nothing happened.

No fall.

No sharp teeth.

No gigantic, chomping jaws.

Instead, Mr. Penguin felt himself moving ever so slowly downward, in a slightly juddery, mechanical fashion.

He dared himself to open one eye. Below him the alligators were still circling, and Miss Bones and Montague were still gripping on to him. Further up, Mr. Penguin couldn't believe what he saw.

The water on either side of him was parting like an enormous pair of soggy curtains, and a rocky platform appeared in between. Mr. Penguin looked at Colin to see if he knew what was going on.

I THINK THIS BRANCH MIGHT ACTUALLY BE A LEVER, he wrote on his pad.

Mr. Penguin watched as the platform slid slowly out from behind the waterfall and came to a grinding stop just under Montague's feet. The gigantic man stepped gently down onto it.

"Well, don't just stand there with your mouth open!" cried Miss Bones. "Help me!"

Montague plucked her down from where she was dangling and then caught Mr. Penguin and placed him onto the platform beside Miss Bones.

Colin quickly untangled Mr. Penguin's satchel from the branch lever and lowered himself down on a web to join the gang. The balcony-like platform led to the entrance of a cave. They all shuffled inside to dry off and gather themselves.

"Phew!" panted Mr. Penguin. "That was lucky! We were almost lunch!" That made him remember his lunch, so he checked his satchel to see how his sandwich was holding up after that unexpected splash in the river. It was slightly soggy on the edges, but it would do. Mr. Penguin popped the satchel over his shoulder and gave it a cheerful pat. "Right!" he said. "What shall we do now? Go back to the museum and dry off?"

CHAPTER FOURTEEN

"Go back to the museum?" Miss Bones cried, emptying river water out of her pumps. "But we haven't found the treasure yet!"

Mr. Penguin's beak fell open. Surely she was joking? "Won't the O'Hoolihan brothers have got it by now? They'll be halfway down Near-The-Park Avenue..."

Of course Mr. Penguin was a little bit disappointed that they'd been beaten to the treasure, but also quite relieved. That business with the alligators had been absolutely terrifying, and all he wanted to do now was sit somewhere warm, dry, and safe and eat his sandwich. Sure, he wouldn't have anything to put in his piggy bank, but maybe that would be okay. *Colin and I could do something else,* he thought. *We could re-advertise ourselves as "Gentle Adventurers" and only solve safe, easy problems...*

He looked at Miss Bones and quickly realized that going somewhere dry and warm for a lunch break wasn't going to happen. She was wringing out her cardigan with her mouth set in a very determined line.

"We MUST find that treasure!" she said firmly. "This museum depends on it!"

She was probably right, thought Mr. Penguin. They'd come this far—it would be silly to give in now and miss the chance of a handsome reward. And they hadn't been in the water that long! Maybe they could still beat the O'Hoolihan brothers to it. He pulled out the map from his satchel and ran his flipper over the dotted red line. He gasped and looked upward, then back at the map.

“Miss Bones!” he cried, grinning his biggest, beakiest grin. “I think we might be in luck! If this cave goes where I think it does, it should lead us directly to where the treasure is hidden! I think we’ve stumbled upon a secret shortcut!”

Miss Bones threw her shoes back on and leapt to her feet. “Then what are we waiting for?”

Colin and Mr. Penguin led the others through the gloomy cave.

“If my calculations are correct,” said

Mr. Penguin after several minutes, "the treasure should be just around this bend..."

They squeezed around the tight, rocky corner one at a time and shuffled into the chamber beyond.

Mr. Penguin blinked.

There in front of them, in two huge treasure chests, were thousands and thousands of gold coins. Glittering among them were diamonds and rubies and sapphires—each the size of one of Montague's fists—as well as gold crowns, silver tiaras, emerald bracelets, and necklaces made from pearls as big as ping-pong balls.

"Look at it all…," said Mr. Penguin in awe. He hardly dared to breathe. "Isn't it just BEAUTIFUL?!"

But before he could say anything else, he felt a sudden, dull wallop on the back of his head. The force threw him to the ground and…

Everything…

went…

BLACK.

CHAPTER FIFTEEN

SEVERAL SERIOUS PROBLEMS

Mr. Penguin opened his eyes and blinked for a few moments.

He was aware of three things:

1. His head felt a bit sore and dizzy—like he'd just come off a tilt-a-whirl or like that time he'd fallen out of the hammock in his igloo.

2. Either the world had turned upside down or he had. He thought about that for a few seconds and decided that it was definitely him who was the wrong way up.

3. He couldn't move. In fact, he was bound up with rope and dangling from his feet, while three hungry alligators waited in the lagoon below, licking their lips menacingly.

He glanced about and saw that Colin was hanging in much the same way beside him.

"What happened?" hissed Mr. Penguin.

Colin shrugged as best he could within the rope, then glanced in the direction of his feet with some alarm. Mr. Penguin followed his gaze and gulped nervously.

They were hanging from the edge of the stone platform in the middle of the waterfall, and the ropes they were dangling from were extremely frayed. Every second, another stringy fiber pinged undone. Soon, it would snap, and Mr. Penguin and Colin would hurtle down into the water and become the alligators' afternoon treat.

Mr. Penguin groaned. This absolutely wasn't how his first Adventure was meant to go. What on earth happened? he wondered. He closed his eyes and desperately tried to remember...

The last thing he was completely sure of was that they had found the treasure. He'd turned around to show Miss Bones and her brother and then—nothing. Nothing at all. He wrinkled his brow, trying to think, and wished that he could untangle one of his flippers so he could scratch his beak. That always helped. Slowly, an idea formed in his mind, and it made his stomach do somersaults with worry.

"Colin!" he hissed. "I think I know what happened! Those jewel thieves followed us to the treasure. They must have crept up behind us, knocked us over the heads with something, and run away with it!"

Colin wiggled about and managed to ping two of his eight legs out of the rope. He scribbled something on his pad: BUT WHAT HAPPENED TO MISS BONES AND HER BROTHER?

As always, Colin made a good point.

Mr. Penguin thought again. "The thieves must have taken them. They've kidnapped Miss Bones and Montague and will ask for a ransom. Then they'll get even MORE money!"

Saying all that aloud made Mr. Penguin

feel very small and silly. Not only had he got himself and his best chum Colin into trouble, but now Miss Bones and Montague were probably tied up somewhere, and all the treasure had been stolen.

The rope creaking and groaning like an old staircase turned his mind to the current problem. How were he and Colin going to escape? Mr. Penguin felt a bit clammy around the bow tie. Any second now, their ropes would snap, and that would be it. The End.

He gulped.

He closed his eyes.

He waited.

Then, all of a sudden, over the roaring sound of the waterfall and the THUMP! THUMP! THUMP! of Mr. Penguin's heart, someone shouted, "Coo-eee!"

CHAPTER SIXTEEN

A WRINKLY FACE

Who could that possibly be? Mr. Penguin snapped open his eyes and looked about. He couldn't believe it. Popping up out of the undergrowth near the lagoon came a wrinkly, smiling face.

It was Edith Hedge! And on her head, as always, was Gordon. He didn't look quite as happy as Edith, but then it was very warm in the jungle, and his feathers seemed a bit frazzled.

"EDITH!" cried Mr. Penguin. "What are YOU doing here?"

Edith didn't say anything but leapt into action as quickly as an elderly lady wearing fifteen coats with a pigeon on her head could manage. She clambered up through the tangle of plants around the lagoon, then disappeared behind the waterfall before appearing again a few moments later, slightly soggy, on the ledge in the middle.

First she hauled Colin up to safety, then together they tried to retrieve Mr. Penguin, but as they pulled...the rope snapped! Edith gasped, Gordon squawked, and Colin's eyes bulged.

As Mr. Penguin fell, one of the hungry alligators leapt up into the air. It opened its huge jaws, but it had misjudged the angle. Instead of landing in its open mouth, Mr. Penguin's head collided with the end of its rubbery snout, and he pinged straight back up into the air!

Colin was ready with a web lasso. He hooked it around Mr. Penguin's feet and dragged him onto the stone ledge. He landed with a very inelegant thud. Edith nimbly untied Mr. Penguin and sat him upright.

"Thank goodness you're safe!" said Edith. "Now we all need to get out of here as quickly as we can. We're in great danger!"

Mr. Penguin straightened his hat. "And we need to go and rescue Miss Bones and her brother from those jewel thieves!"

Edith suddenly looked very serious. "But, Mr. Penguin," she said, "Boudicca Bones hasn't got a brother. I think you've been tricked!"

CHAPTER SEVENTEEN

OH BROTHER!

"What?" cried Mr. Penguin. He stumbled backward toward the edge. Edith caught him by the satchel just in time. "I don't understand…"

"Miss Bones hasn't got a brother!" repeated Edith. "I knew something wasn't right this morning when I saw that the museum was closed. Then you told me about the treasure hunt. I thought, like you said, that was the reason the place was all shut up. But when you left, I went back to the park with Gordon, and I couldn't shake that funny feeling I had. I thought back over everything, and I remembered you saying that Miss Bones AND HER BROTHER had asked you to come and find the missing treasure. Well, Miss Bones doesn't have a brother! She doesn't even have a sister! I've known her since she was a baby. I even knew her mum and dad. I used to chat to them when they were pushing her around the duck pond in the park. I realized you could be in a lot of danger. So I followed you."

Mr. Penguin couldn't believe his ears. It all sounded completely bonkers! A hundred different questions bounced around his brain, but before he could ask any of them, Colin held up his pad.

SO IT WAS YOU WE HEARD CLONKING AND THUMPING AT THE DOOR TO COME IN?

It was now Edith's turn to look confused.

"Clonking and thumping at the door?" she said. "No, that wasn't me. I just picked the lock with this. Easy as anything!" She pulled a large hairpin from her belt bag and held it up proudly. "But when I got in, you'd all disappeared down here. Gordon and I had to come down those blummin' steps in the pitch black and then, of course, we were too late again. The four of you had disappeared into this jungle. I had to keep sending Gordon up high to see where you were going, and then I followed his directions, didn't I, Gord?"

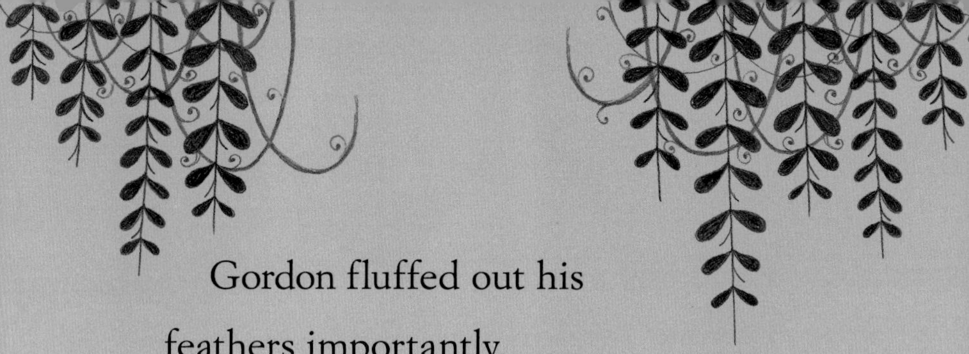

Gordon fluffed out his feathers importantly.

"I don't move as quickly as I used to," Edith continued, "so all these plants were quite tricky to climb over. Especially in my slippers..."

She waggled her feet. She was indeed wearing her slippers—grubby pink ones with fluffy edging and huge red pom-poms on the toes. "When I DID catch up with you, you'd just got onto that alligator's back. I knew it wasn't a log, but I didn't dare shout to warn you, as I thought Miss Bones and her 'brother' might feed you to that beast.

“Then you all went over the waterfall, and I thought that was it. I thought that was the end of my lovely Mr. Penguin and Colin! I couldn’t believe it when you were saved by the branch! I hurried to try to catch up with you, but you’d gone into that cave. I couldn’t get there before I saw Miss Bones and her brother leaving it. He had two great big treasure chests on his shoulders, and Miss Bones was dragging you and Colin out.”

Mr. Penguin’s eyes were like saucers as he tried to keep up with it all. “It must have been her!” he cried. “She must have walloped us over the head with her handbag!”

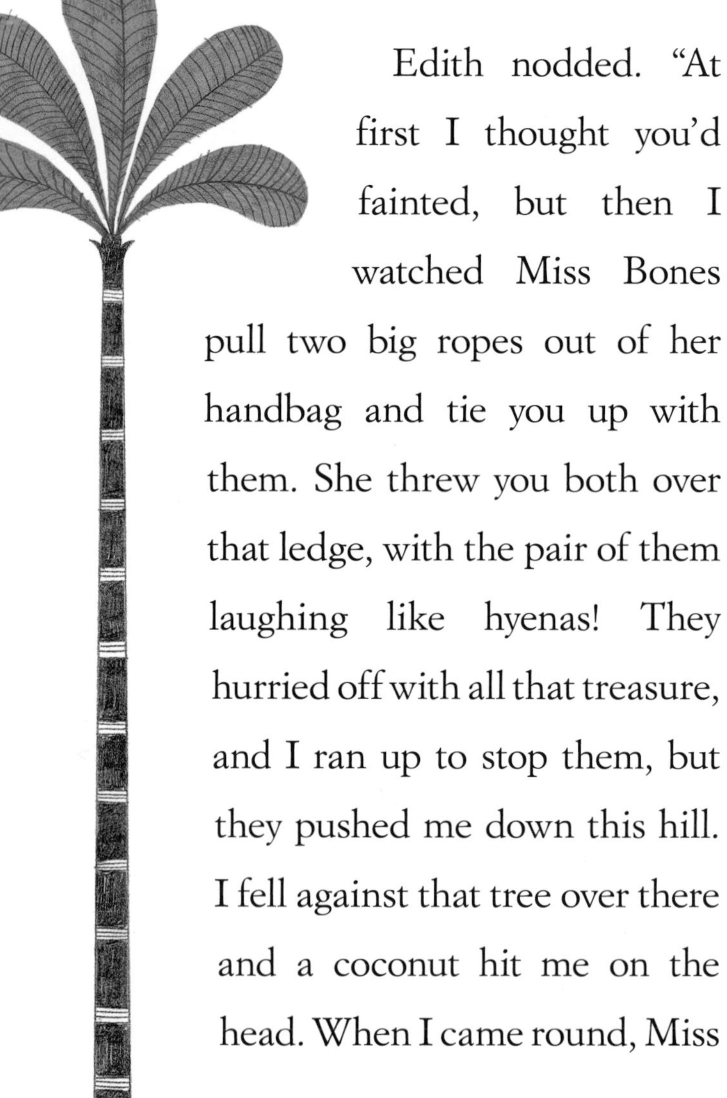

Edith nodded. "At first I thought you'd fainted, but then I watched Miss Bones pull two big ropes out of her handbag and tie you up with them. She threw you both over that ledge, with the pair of them laughing like hyenas! They hurried off with all that treasure, and I ran up to stop them, but they pushed me down this hill. I fell against that tree over there and a coconut hit me on the head. When I came round, Miss

Bones and that man were nowhere to be seen!"

"But we'd been helping her!" said Mr. Penguin. "Why would she do such a thing?"

"I don't know," sighed Edith. "But I think there's something fishy about it all. Miss Bones looked different somehow. Not how I remember her at all..."

Mr. Penguin flapped his flippers and shook his head to clear his thoughts. As the cogs in his brain whirred at supersonic speed, he felt like a puzzle was coming together—he just needed the last piece for it all to make sense. But what was it?

The main question was, if Miss Bones didn't have a brother, then who was Montague? That was the key. Brother... brothers...

The final piece of the puzzle suddenly slotted into place, and Mr. Penguin clapped his flippers to his head. "Do you have your newspaper with you?" he asked Edith.

"Of course!" said Edith, ferreting about in her belt bag. "But why?"

Mr. Penguin took it from her and laid it on the floor. He pointed to a photograph on the cover.

"You see," said Mr. Penguin, "I don't think for a minute we've been helping the real Miss Bones at all. In fact, I'd bet your belt bag on it! Look!"

Edith, Colin, and Gordon studied the photograph of two villainous-looking men. They shrugged at Mr. Penguin. What WAS he going on about?

Mr. Penguin took his pencil out of his satchel and started to draw on top of the photograph. He drew a skinny mustache on Rory, the tall one, and scribbled some hair, glasses, and lipstick on Brian, the small, round one.

Edith yelped.

Colin GASPED in capital letters.

Gordon didn't say anything, but then he was generally unflappable.

got up q
osphere amongst
zoo dwellers.

ESCAPED PRISONE
STILL AT LARGE

Cityville cops are contin
hunt for two priso
o broke free
ville County
ty Jail two nights
s Brian 'The
ory
O'

F
the
the
compr
and ma
to the wi
Workers

thought to ha
tunnelli
wall

"'Miss Bones' and her 'brother' are none other than Brian and Rory O'Hoolihan!" said Mr. Penguin. "THEY are the jewel thieves in disguise!"

CHAPTER EIGHTEEN

MR. PENGUIN HAS A PLAN

"What a silly, silly, SILLY penguin I've been!" Mr. Penguin groaned, flopping down onto the floor.

"How did I not see all this before? I was too excited for our first Adventuring case that I never thought for a minute that we could be tricked. Now I've lost the treasure and put everyone in danger Goodness knows where the REAL Miss Bones is."

He covered his face with his hat and groaned again.

Meanwhile, Edith was thinking aloud. "I think those O'Hoolihan boys will still be trekking through this jungle. It'll be hard going with two heavy treasure chests to carry. We can still catch them—but we'd better get cracking now!"

Mr. Penguin didn't move. He was too fed up.

"Come on now, Mr. Penguin!" said Edith, firmly. "This isn't at all how a real Adventurer would behave! There's still a chance for you to save the day!"

Mr. Penguin thought about it. He supposed that was true. In his favorite book, there was always a way for the Adventurer to save the day. He didn't give up just because he was being shot at with poisoned arrows or about to be thrown into a shark tank. He fought on and kept going. And that was what Mr. Penguin was going to do!

He leapt to his feet, put his hat back on, straightened his bow tie, and grabbed the map out of his satchel. The O'Hoolihans had been too stupid to think of stealing that, he thought with a grin.

But then his heart began to sink again. "The tunnel back up to the museum is a really long way from here along the path. We'll never catch up with the thieves that way."

Mr. Penguin scanned the map again—the river ran in great, wiggly loops all around the underground jungle, coming very close to where he had found the treasure map in the first place. Just by the tunnel that led up to the museum!

"If only we had a boat," he said, rubbing his beak thoughtfully, "we could sail down the river and be back at that tunnel in a few minutes! We might even beat the O'Hoolihan brothers to it!"

BUT WE DON'T HAVE A BOAT, Colin's pad read.

This was true, but Mr. Penguin had a little itch of an idea.

He reached into his satchel to check if his packed lunch was still there. It was! Then he looked over into the lagoon below at the three gigantic alligators splashing about.

His idea was a dangerous one, and it would involve a bit of a sacrifice, but it might just work…

CHAPTER NINETEEN

HOW NOT TO BE EATEN BY AN ALLIGATOR

Five minutes later, Mr. Penguin, Colin, Edith, and Gordon were whizzing down the river on the back of one of the alligators. Mr. Penguin's plan had worked perfectly, with not even one accidentally-being-eaten part in it.

Colin had hopped down and biffed all the beasts except one on the nose to jolly well show them who was boss. They'd splashed back into the shadows with their tails between their legs.

Then Mr. Penguin had taken his (now squashed and soggy) fish finger sandwich out of his satchel and waggled it in the air at the last alligator. It had liked the smell of that. It had liked the smell a lot! So much so that, as Mr. Penguin passed the sandwich to Colin, this alligator let Mr. Penguin, Edith, and Gordon clamber onto its back without even trying to nibble one of them. Its eyes were too busy watching the sandwich Colin was holding.

Colin and the sandwich then climbed aboard and dangled themselves just in front of the alligator's nose from a stick Mr. Penguin was holding. With the fish finger sandwich enticing it forward, the alligator had launched off from the banks of the lagoon with the gang onboard.

"Can you see anything?" cried Mr. Penguin, holding on to the sandwich stick as tightly as possible with his flippers. Colin gave the alligator a warning bop on the nose with a kung fu kick as it got a bit too close to the sandwich. Edith and Gordon scanned the jungle for signs of the O'Hoolihan brothers.

"Nothing!" yelled Edith over the noise of the alligator's splashing legs. "Nothing apart from some trampled plants—so we must be going the right way!"

The alligator swung around the bend of the river, and Mr. Penguin saw from his map that they were now in the right place. He waggled the stick to the left, and Colin and the sandwich led the alligator to the edge of the water. Everyone hopped off.

Mr. Penguin helped Colin off the stick, then threw his lunch to the alligator, who swallowed it down in one enormous gulp and grinned widely before swimming off. It was the least he could do seeing as the alligator had been so helpful and hadn't eaten them.

Mr. Penguin watched it swim away. Sacrificing his sandwich for the treasure was obviously the right thing to do, but it was still difficult to think that he wouldn't get to eat it…

"Come on!" said Edith. "Stop dilly-dallying!"

Mr. Penguin straightened his hat and scrabbled up the rest of the bank to the sandy ground by the entrance to the tunnel.

The O'Hoolihan brothers were nowhere in sight.

Mr. Penguin pulled his giant magnifying glass out of his satchel. He spotted some fresh footprints running out of the jungle toward the tunnel entrance, and a gold coin, partly covered in sand.

"We've missed them!" said Mr. Penguin, but Colin was holding up his pad.

I CAN HEAR SOMETHING, it said.

They all listened. Colin was right. They could definitely hear something.

It was coming from above them—the sound of gruff male voices and the jangling of jewels.

"Quick!" cried Mr. Penguin. "We aren't too late! They're still in the museum!"

And he ran into the tunnel, followed by his three best friends.

CHAPTER TWENTY

CAUGHT IN THE ACT

The tunnel was harder work on the way up than it had been on the way down. It spiraled around and around at quite a dizzying rate. The walls still beetled and shimmered with hundreds of insects, but Mr. Penguin didn't think about them.

He HAD to reach the museum before the O'Hoolihans escaped.

He edged up the slippery, uneven steps and around the corners as fast as his two short penguin-y legs could carry him. Not far behind, Colin scuttled and Edith Hedge shuffled as best she could in her bedroom slippers. Gordon ruffled his feathers and gripped onto Edith's headscarf tightly with his feet.

Eventually, they all spilled out onto the museum floor.

It was now night. An inky black sky covered the domed glass ceiling, and rain hammered down on it relentlessly.

"Ha!" said a gruff, sneering voice. "If it isn't our friend Mr. Penguin and his gang of idiots! I didn't think we'd be seeing YOU again…well, not all in one piece at least!"

A harsh, gravelly laugh echoed through the room. Mr. Penguin looked around to find the voice. It came from Miss Bones, or rather Brian "The Brain" O'Hoolihan, notorious jewel thief. His brother, Rory "Knuckles" O'Hoolihan, was chuckling beside him. The pair of them stood in the middle of the room, surrounded by the treasure. Brian was directing Rory in the task of stuffing it all into sacks—easier to escape with, Mr. Penguin guessed.

Brian grinned evilly at the newcomers. He looked quite different now, having thrown off the strawberry blonde wig he'd been wearing as Miss Bones. His own wispy, sweaty strands of hair were standing bolt upright from his greasy forehead. His red lipstick was smeared right across his mouth and flabby cheeks, and his smudged eye shadow made him look like a crazy panda. His chin was covered in blue-gray stubble and a fat, hairy knee poked out from a large hole in one of his stockings.

Beside him, Rory looked equally ridiculous. He'd obviously got too hot carrying the treasure, so he'd rolled up the legs of his trousers to make an improvised pair of shorts, and ripped the arms off his shirt. He was flexing the muscles of his thick, tattooed arms menacingly.

At a nod from his brother, Rory cracked his knuckles and lumbered toward Mr. Penguin and his friends until they were all pressed up against the wall. Something jabbed Mr. Penguin uncomfortably in the back, but he didn't dare look. With a snarl, Rory returned to the treasure and carried on filling his bag.

"You won't get away with this!" said Mr. Penguin, hoping that he sounded as brave as the hero in his favorite Adventure book. But it came out sounding strangled, which made Brian O'Hoolihan laugh again, and

he elbowed his brother in the thigh until Rory joined in too.

"Oh PLEASE, Mr. Penguin!" Brian roared. "Please tell me what you think you're going to do about it all? To be honest with you, I can't quite believe we've got this far! I thought you might see through my disguise, but of course you didn't. It was unbelievable—you just took in everything I told you! Now, you're obviously not COMPLETELY stupid—you did help us with that annoying clue to lead us to the treasure, but not without almost getting us eaten on the way. But no matter how clever you think you are, Mr. Penguin, I will ALWAYS be cleverer. I shall always remember that lovely sound of me clonking you over the head with my handbag..."

As Brian spoke, Mr. Penguin reached behind his back to try to work out what was jabbing him.

"I knew full well we should have just thrown you and that RIDICULOUS spider friend of yours straight to the 'gators," Brian continued, putting a fistful of coins into his handbag, "but I couldn't resist a little bit of drama. The thought of you waking up just as you fell into the water to be eaten was so gloriously amusing to me. I should have liked to have watched it, but we did need to get on. We have a flight to catch out of the country, and all this treasure is coming with us!"

"No, it isn't!" Mr. Penguin shouted crossly. "That treasure belongs to the REAL Miss Bones and the museum!"

Brian O'Hoolihan guffawed. "Come on then!" he shouted. "What are you going to do? What can a penguin, a spider, and an old woman with a pigeon on her head do to stop us—the greatest thieves the world has ever seen?"

He roared with laughter again and tied up one of the sacks with a neat little bow. Then he turned his back on them and whistled to his brother. Rory heaved the sacks up and they headed toward the door.

"You see, Mr. Penguin," called Brian over his shoulder, "you are stupid and pathetic. There's nothing you can do to stop us!"

Mr. Penguin quickly glanced at his friends. He winked at Colin.

Colin grinned.

Mr. Penguin cleared his throat. “Well,” he said, “we CAN do this…”

CHAPTER TWENTY-ONE

LET'S GET OUTTA HERE!

Mr. Penguin reached up behind him and, with all his might, wrenched the water pipe that had been sticking into his back off the wall. At the same time, he elbowed an alarm button by his flipper, and it started to scream like a baby. Hundreds of gallons of water sloshed out across the floor.

The O'Hoolihan brothers hadn't expected that.

Rory O'Hoolihan squealed a high-pitched squeal, dropped the sacks of treasure, and tried desperately to stop his feet from slipping out from under him. Brian O'Hoolihan's face turned scarlet.

"PICK UP THOSE BAGS, YOU IDIOT!" he yelled. "AND LET'S GET OUTTA HERE!"

Rory did as he was told and the two crooks began hoofing it across the slippery floor.

Edith put two fingers to her lips and blew an ear-piercing whistle. Gordon launched himself off her head and headed straight for the thieves like an arrow. Screeching furiously, Gordon swooped and pecked at the brothers' ears and noses, diving into them over and over again until they were a blur of flying fists and feathers.

"GET THIS STINKING, FLYING RAT OFF ME!" roared Brian over the noise, but Gordon didn't give up, and the two brothers stumbled and slid their way across the room.

Mr. Penguin gave Colin the nod.

The spider squared his jaw, leapt up, and kicked off from the wall. As he flew through the air, he shot out a long line of web from his bottom, throwing it so that the end knotted around a gas pipe running along the baseboard. Colin landed and pulled the web tight to create a nearly invisible string that stretched across the room.

Just at that moment, the two brothers came tumbling toward it. With Gordon flinging himself into their faces, they didn't see the trip wire until it was too late. They went crashing and skidding across the tiles, circling twice around the dinosaur skeleton before sliding to a stop. Mr. Penguin waddled calmly over to the panting brothers.

When he reached the final bone of the

dinosaur's tail, Mr. Penguin gave it a light push with his flipper, and the entire skeleton began to shake. As it wobbled above their heads the two brothers tried desperately to get to their feet. But water was still gushing out of the pipe, mixing with all the dust in the room and covering the floor with a thick, slippery goo.

It was useless. The crooks fell to the ground just as the skeleton broke loose from its supporting cables. It tumbled down on top of the squealing brothers, trapping them inside its ancient rib cage.

When the dust had settled, Mr. Penguin bent down to look through the bars of the skeletal prison.

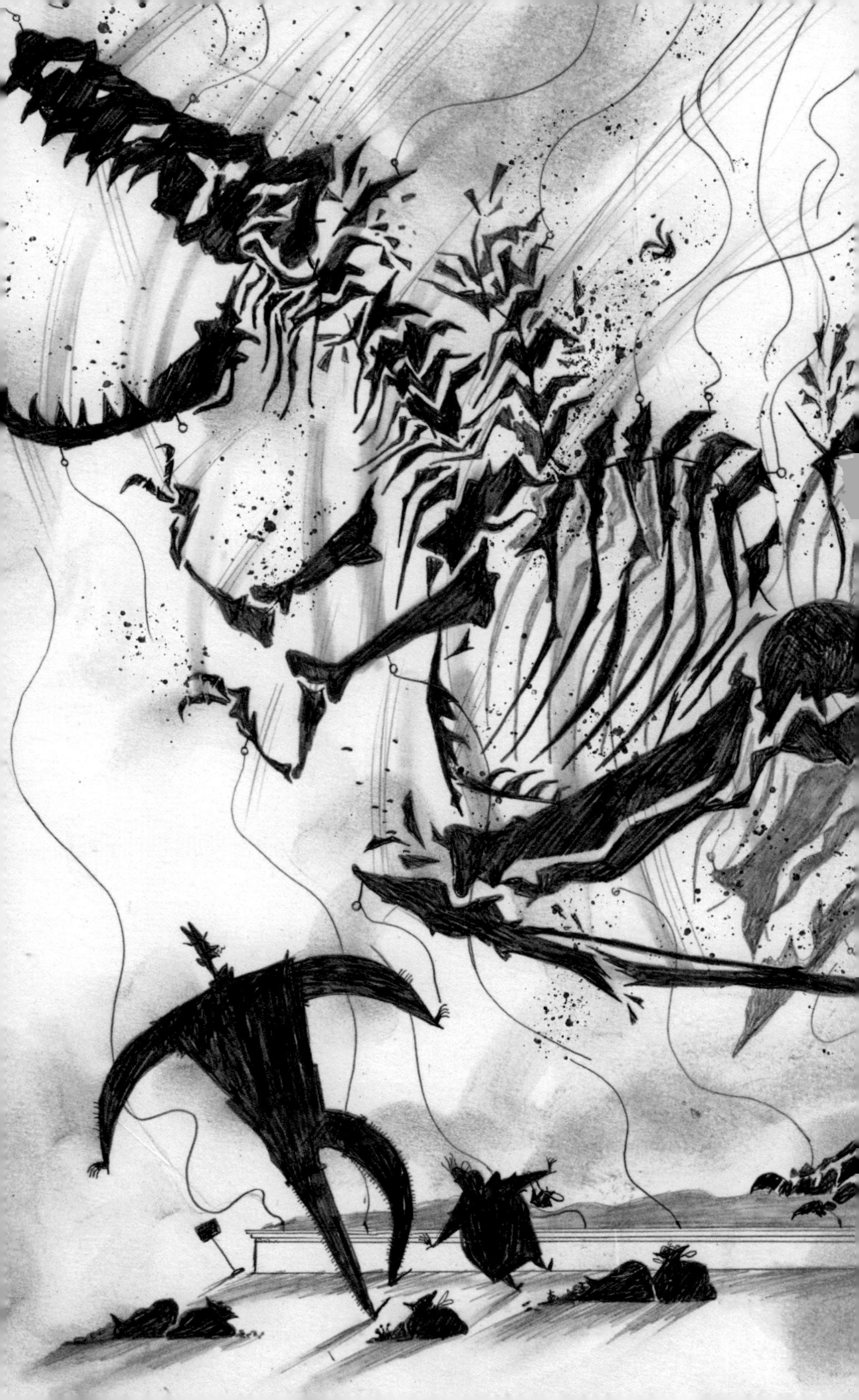

"Don't ever underestimate old ladies!" laughed Edith Hedge.

"Or penguins!" cried Mr. Penguin.

OR COLINS, said Colin's pad.

Gordon didn't say anything.

Inside the dinosaur, the prisoners bent their soggy heads in shame as the sound of sirens and screeching police cars, alerted by the ringing alarm, filled the air from the courtyard outside.

CHAPTER TWENTY-TWO

A FISH FINGER SANDWICH (AT LAST!)

It was nearly midnight, and Alf couldn't remember a time when his restaurant had been so busy. Every seat in the Popular Plaice 24-Hour Diner was taken by men and women brandishing notepads and pens.

Every few seconds bright camera flashes went off, lighting the place up like a fireworks display. It was extraordinary!

Nobody was looking at Alf though. All eyes were on the odd collection of grubby characters sitting in a booth surrounded by bags of glittering treasure. There was Mr. Penguin, covered in mud and dust but grinning happily. He held a fish finger sandwich in his flipper and had ketchup splodged all around his beak. Next to him, Colin slurped a mug of black, treacly coffee. Edith Hedge, still wearing all her coats and belt bag, sat on the other side of Mr. Penguin, eating a slice of cherry pie and ice cream. Every so often she tossed a handful of pastry up to Gordon, who cooed contentedly on her head. Finally, at the end of the row, was a tall woman with strawberry-blonde, slightly bedraggled hair. She had big, kind blue eyes and was talking excitedly to everyone and waving her hands about. This was the real Miss Bones.

"Well," she said in her nice, tinkly voice, "it all started for me two nights ago. I was working late in my office, as I often do. I was cataloging a collection of clockwork crystal cats when I heard a window shatter on the ground floor. I went to investigate, but there was nobody there. Then out of the shadows came the O'Hoolihan brothers. I knew it was them—like they told Mr. Penguin, Brian O'Hoolihan had been writing to me for months, wanting to know about the objects in the museum, and then about the treasure."

She held up the copy of *A History of the Museum of Extraordinary Objects* the fake Miss Bones had given Mr. Penguin in the museum. A shimmer of camera flashes went off as everyone clamored to take pictures of it.

"They tied me to a chair in my office and questioned me for ages about the book they'd found in the prison library.

OUR FISH FINGERS ARE FAMOUS!

They thought I wasn't telling the truth when I said I knew nothing about the treasure. But I'd never seen the book before, and I only knew about the history of the museum from bits and pieces my family had told me. My great-great-great-grandfather, Sir Randolph Bones, was by all accounts a very brilliant but eccentric man. He spent his life traveling the world collecting extraordinary objects and strange animals and plants, and bringing them back here to Cityville for his museum. There was a story that he'd once managed to recover two treasure chests that had been hidden on a desert island by a fearsome pirate, but everyone thought that was just what it was—a story." She waved a hand over the glittering coins and jewels in front of her. "But now…it appears to have been absolutely true!"

There was another chorus of camera pops and flashes.

"I've been told that Sir Randolph was forever tinkering about in the basement of the museum, but nobody had a clue what he was up to. When he died at the age of 102, an inspection revealed nothing. He must have built a fake basement to hide his real work—a laboratory full of the exotic plants and animals he'd discovered on his travels, not to mention the hiding place of his treasure. He must have been

terrifically worried that the pirate would come back and try to retrieve his loot! But instead of a pirate, it was the O'Hoolihans who became obsessed by it. When I couldn't give them any answers, they tied me up, put a filthy handkerchief in my mouth, and locked me in a cupboard. THAT was the clonking and thumping you could hear, Colin—me trying to get out!"

Poor Miss Bones, thought Mr. Penguin, remembering how relieved she'd looked when they'd found her in the cupboard.

"All I could hear was those two dreadful crooks tearing through my museum," Miss

Bones continued. "The mess the museum is in now is because of them. They pulled everything apart, smashed holes in the walls with sledgehammers, and even pulled the trees in the garden up with their bare hands. This treasure will help pay to put all of that right again, and the police chief said she'll bring those crooks back to the museum tomorrow morning and will personally see to it that they clean up all the mess they've made. Then I will open up the jungle beneath the museum for the public—once we have the alligators under control, of course! Mr. Penguin has given me some tips on how to do that!"

Mr. Penguin grinned and waggled his fish finger sandwich in the air.

The journalists laughed and scribbled all this down furiously while the cameras flashed and popped.

Miss Bones turned to the gang of Adventurers beside her and placed her hand gently on Mr. Penguin's shoulders. "I'd like to say an enormous thank-you to Edith, to Gordon, to Colin, and to my dear, dear Mr. Penguin. Without your cleverness, bravery, and super Adventuring spirit, this treasure would now be on its way out of the country with those two horrible thieves, and I would still be locked in that cupboard! And as a token of my thanks for everything you've done for the museum, I would like to present you with these." She gave them each a heavy cloth bag, full to the brim with golden coins and jewels.

At this, the diner broke out in thunderous applause and cheering, and the cameras flashed again. Alf found himself mopping away a tear with his dishcloth.

In among noise, Mr. Penguin looked down at his bag of treasure and grinned. These gold coins will certainly pay for an awful lot of fish finger sandwiches, he thought happily, and I can stay nice and warm and dry in my igloo home in Cityville.

CHAPTER TWENTY-THREE

HOME

The city was waking up by the time Mr. Penguin and Colin got back to their igloo. The sun was just peeking up above the roofs of the skyscrapers and sparkling off their windows. It made the entire town look like it was covered in sequins.

On their way home, the two friends had stopped by a newspaper stand and were amazed to see themselves grinning out from the front covers of all the early editions. Newspapers were flying off the shelves as everyone in Cityville scrambled to get the full story about the incredible night at the museum.

The two Adventurers were exhausted. Their first case had turned out to be more exciting than Mr. Penguin could have ever imagined.

Once inside their igloo, Colin YAWN-ED loudly on his pad then wrote GOOD NIGHT and clambered into the third drawer of the filing cabinet.

Mr. Penguin carefully slotted his gold coins into his piggy bank before hanging up his hat and satchel. Then he climbed sleepily up the ladder to his hammock.

He kicked off his shoes and yawned so widely his face almost disappeared.

Yes, he thought to himself as he snuggled down under his covers, that was a very exciting day indeed. What he needed now was a long sleep and later he would probably find room for another fish finger sandwich or two. That made him feel very happy, and he wiggled his feet cheerfully under his blanket.

But just as he closed his eyes and got ready for a good sleep, the telephone rang.

And on the end of it was another exciting Adventure!

THE END

(Until next time…)

The Cityville Times

MORNING EDITION

5th OCTOBER

MR. PENGUIN SAVES THE DAY!

LOST TREASURE FOUND

HIDDEN JUNGLE DISCOVERED

ESCAPED CROOKS BACK IN PRISON

New Heroes in town! Colin (left) and Mr. Penguin (right) pose with some of the newly discovered, priceless pirate loot.

There were dramatic scenes in Cityville last night, when The Museum of Extraordinary Objects found itself under attack from a pair of dastardly thieves who were set on making off with a priceless collection of pirate treasure. Escaped convicts Brian "The Brain" and Rory O'Hoolihan are now back in police custody thanks to the brave efforts of some Cityville residents.

Mr. Penguin, Adventurer and Penguin, along with his assistant Colin, had been called in by the Museum's director, Miss Boudicca Bones, to help her to find some hidden treasure. It wasn't until much later that the two fearless adventurers discovered that they had been duped, and that the real Miss Bones was actually tied up in a cupboard, and they were, in fact, working for the two crooks—both heavily disguised! Despite some death-defying set-backs—including a run-in with a newly uncovered breed of giant alligators, Mr. Penguin and Colin, along with their friends Edith Hedge and Gordon, managed to save the treasure, catch the crooks and free Miss Bones from her cupboard.

FULL IN-DEPTH LOOK AT THE CASE ON PAGES 2–7 INSIDE.

REGISTRATION IS NOW OPEN FOR THE 32nd BIANNUAL INTERNATIONAL RODENT FESTIVAL!

Registration form on page 10

Acknowledgments

A BIG THANK-YOU ALSO TO REBECCA LOGAN and DANIEL FRICKER for their enthusiastic support of Mr. Penguin and Colin.

FURTHER THANKS TO

… McNEIL, ALISON …EY, RACHEL BODEN, …YN FRANCIS and …LINE THOMSON, the fantastic team at …tte UK HQ.

ENORMOUS THANK-YOU TO

EMMA LAYFIELD, for her expert editing.

ALISON STILL, for her wonderful design skills.

ALISON ELDRED, agent extraordinaire and honorary Adventurer.

Thank-you to **DAVID JAMES LENNON** for organising a meet-and-greet with real penguins for research purposes.

MUSEUM NEEDS YOUR HELP!

As a result of last night's adventures in the museum, an enormous clean-up operation is needed to get the place back to its former glory, and YOU can help!

Museum Director Miss Boudicca Bones says: "We really are looking for all hands on deck to get the museum looking ship-shape again. Many objects—including our giant T-Rex skeleton—have been broken so we are looking for any Cityville citizens with a free half an hour and some sticky tape to come and give us a hand."

Miss Bones then went on to say that as a thank-you, free entry would be given to any volunteers for the new Underground Jungle and Treasure-Hunting Tour which will open in the coming months, or, as Miss Bones said: "As soon as we've got the alligators under control!"